see

...ng stars that twinkled ...nick, glittering mist. Out beyond the c..., she could hear the whoops and cries and hoots of different animals. As she stared out into the darkness she had the same feeling she'd had earlier – that she was being watched. She heard the crack of twigs and stiffened. Was something there?

Halisi nudged her and nodded towards the trees. "Elephant," he said softly.

"Out there?" Emily said in delight.

"Yes. Just one. It is quiet. It watches us but it will pass by."

Emily saw the shadows move. She wished she could see the elephant. Then she heard a faint noise, a gentle trumpeting. She looked at Halisi, her eyes wide.

"The elephant. I think it says *jambo*," he said with a smile.

Meet all of Emily's

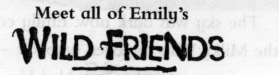

WILD FRIENDS

ELEPHANTS NEVER FORGET

By Linda Chapman and Michelle Misra

Illustrated by Rob McPhillips

RED FOX

WWF WILD FRIENDS: ELEPHANTS NEVER FORGET

A RED FOX BOOK 978 1 849 41694 8

First Published in Great Britain by Red Fox,
an imprint of Random House Children's Publishers UK
A Random House Group Company

This edition published 2013

1 3 5 7 9 10 8 6 4 2

Random House Children's Publishers UK uses the WWF marks under license from
WWF–World Wide Fund for Nature. WWF is not the manufacturer of this product.

WWF-UK is a charity reg'd in England and Wales (no. 1081247) and in Scotland
(no. SC039593) and relies on support from its members and the public. This product is
produced under license from WWF-UK (World Wide Fund for Nature) Trading Limited,
Godalming, Surrey, GU7 1XR. Thank you for your help.

The Random House Group Limited supports the Forest Stewardship Council (FSC®),
the leading international forest certification organization. Our books carrying the FSC label
are printed on FSC®-certified paper. FSC is the only forest certification scheme
endorsed by the leading environmental organizations, including Greenpeace.
Our paper procurement policy can be found at www.randomhouse.co.uk/environment.

MIX
Paper from
responsible sources
FSC® C016897
www.fsc.org

Set in Bembo MT
Red Fox Books are published by Random House Children's Publishers UK,
61–63 Uxbridge Road, London W5 5SA

www.**randomhousechildrens**.co.uk
www.**randomhouse**.co.uk

Addresses for companies within The Random House Group Limited
can be found at: www.randomhouse.co.uk/offices.htm

THE RANDOM HOUSE GROUP Limited Reg. No. 954009

A CIP catalogue record for this book is available from the British Library.

Printed and bound by CPI Group (UK) Ltd, Croydon, CR0 4YY

**Turn to page 77 for lots
of information on WWF,
plus some cool activities!**

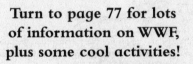

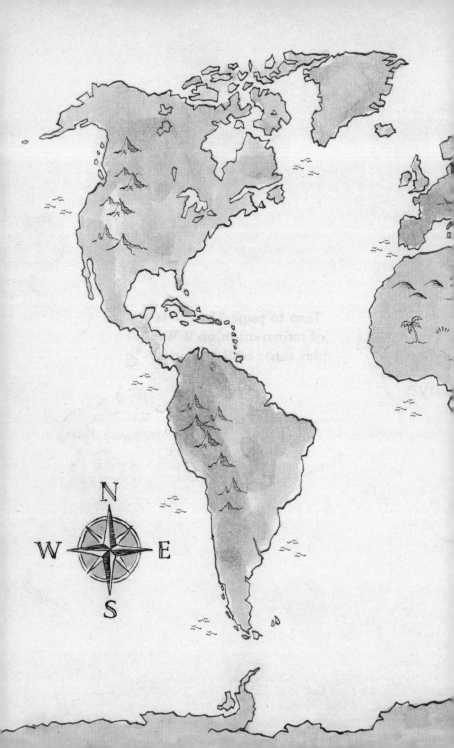

enya

One Week to Go

The rain poured. Emily Oliver sat by the window, watching the drops race each other down the glass pane. Outside, the world looked grey. All the animals and birds in the garden were sheltering in the trees. Emily could hardly believe that in just a week's time she would be in Kenya, a very hot country in Africa. Excitement tingled through her. Loads of different wild animals lived there — lions, giraffes, zebras, cheetahs, gazelle, buffalo — and best of all, *elephants*!

Emily loved all animals, but she particularly liked elephants with their wrinkly grey skin, big flapping ears and kind, wise eyes. *I wonder if I'll meet one,* she thought. She had been to all sorts of amazing places because her mum and dad worked for WWF, an organization that helped protect animals and their habitats around the world. Emily's mum was a photographer and her dad helped set up WWF projects in different countries. But this trip was different – this time they were going on holiday. And not just any holiday – on safari!

They were going to fly to the capital of Kenya, Nairobi, and then stay a night with one of her mum and dad's friends who worked for WWF, before travelling the next day to the Masai Mara Nature Reserve. It would take them a few hours by minibus to get there, but Emily didn't mind. She had never been on safari before and she couldn't wait!

She wandered around the room, feeling restless – she wished she was already in Kenya! Her eyes fell on a collection of photo albums on the bookcase. They were full of her mum's photos from around the world. All the covers were labelled and many of them were from before Emily had been born. As Emily began to look through them, she wondered if there were any with photos of Africa in them.

Australia . . . India . . . Russia . . . Her eyes skipped over the different labels and then saw one that said *Kenya*. She pulled it out of the pile and opened it up.

There were photos of her mum and dad

standing by a
river full of hippos.
They were with
some other people
and a toddler
with dark curly
hair in bunches.
Emily frowned.
It looked like her, but had she ever been to
Kenya? She didn't think so. Still, she had
definitely looked like that when she was a
toddler.

She turned the page of the album and
gasped out loud as she saw dozens of
photos of elephants. There were elephants
bathing at a watering hole, elephants
spraying water over themselves, elephants
twining trunks. And then she saw a close-
up photo of a young elephant. It was
touching the toddler's tummy with its trunk
and she was touching its grey wrinkled

cheek. They were
gazing at each
other, completely
ignoring the
camera. The
toddler was
smiling and if
elephants could

smile, this one would have been smiling
back. Was it really her in the photo?

Just then the door opened and her mum
came in. "Gran's going to make a cake. She
said do you want to come and help her?"

"Look, Mum." Emily waved the photo
album at her. "I found these. Is this me?
Have I been to Kenya before?"

Her mum's dark hair was loose around
her shoulders. She tucked it behind her ears
as she looked at the photos. "Yes. You were
about two years old then." She smiled, as
if remembering. "It was your first big trip

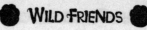

abroad. I travelled out there to take some photos in the Masai Mara and you and Dad came with me. That was when we got to know Abasi, whose flat we'll be staying at this time. I'd forgotten you'd been there with us."

Emily pointed to the photo of the elephant tickling her tummy with its trunk. "Look at this!"

Her mum smiled fondly. "I remember that! Weren't you cute? That elephant had been orphaned and was really shy and reserved with people and other elephants, but she took a real shine to you. Maybe it was because you were so small. She used to call out to you and you would make a noise back. Then she'd follow you around and touch your hair and tickle your tummy with her trunk. You used to say she was a heffalant. I suppose you could say she was your very first wild friend."

Emily stared at the picture of the young elephant with intelligent eyes. She wished she could remember meeting her. "What was she called?"

Her mum scratched her head. "It began with a K. Let me see . . ." She looked at the photo again. "Kihari!" she said suddenly. "That was it. She was about five years old."

Emily knew that elephant babies usually drank their mother's milk until they were about four, and then they stayed with their mums, living in a small group of females called a herd. She also knew that elephants were really sociable animals. They helped each other, liked to play and had very good memories. Emily looked at the photo of her and the elephant. "Is Kihari still alive?"

"I imagine so," her mum said. "Elephants

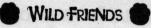

usually live until they're about sixty-five, if
nothing bad happens to them. We're going
back to the same place where you met her
last time. Maybe we'll see her!"

"I hope so," said Emily. She touched
the elephant in the photo with one finger.
Would the elephant still remember her? It
was about eight years ago, so Kihari would
be thirteen years old by now, but she knew
elephants were never supposed to forget
anything.

Kihari. She said the name in her head.
She really hoped she would see her very
first wild friend again!

Arriving in Nairobi

The week flew by. In no time at all, school
was over and Emily and her parents found
themselves on an aeroplane heading to
Nairobi. It was an eight-hour flight and
Emily fell asleep after a few hours. She
woke up just as the plane was starting
to descend. Blinking and stretching, she
looked out of the window. Beneath them
were rolling green and brown plains. Rivers
snaked across the ground, shining silver in
the sun. It was so bright outside that it hurt
Emily's eyes. It looked like it was really hot
too. She was suddenly glad that she was

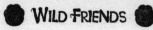

wearing shorts, even though it had been damp and chilly in England when they had got on the plane, and she'd been keeping her coat over her bare legs so she didn't get cold. As they flew lower her ears felt funny and she swallowed to try and help the pressure.

"Do you want a sweet?" her dad asked, noticing.

"Yes, please."

He handed her a big bag of fruit sherbets and as she started sucking on one, her ears felt a bit better. Her dad smiled at her. "Are you feeling excited?"

"Oh, yes!" Emily's eyes shone. "I can't wait to go on safari and see the elephants!"

"I've got an elephant joke," her dad said.

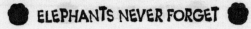

"What is it?" Emily asked cautiously. Her dad's jokes were usually not very good.

"What's big and grey and protects you from the rain?"

"I don't know, Dad," said Emily. "What's big and grey and protects you from the rain?"

"An umbr*ellaphant*!" her dad declared.

Emily groaned. "Dad! That's awful!"

"All right. How about this one? Why were the elephants thrown out of the swimming pool?"

"Why?"

"Because they couldn't keep their trunks up!"

Emily shook her head and tried not to smile, but then she caught her dad's eye and they both started to giggle.

"Enough elephant jokes, you two!" her mum said. "Look, we're coming down to land!"

The airport was busy with people
everywhere – pushing trolleys, standing
in queues, wheeling suitcases along and
buying things from lots of little shops.
The Olivers collected their bags from the
conveyor belt and made their way through
to the exit. They found a man holding up a
cardboard sign with their name on. He was
a taxi driver who was going to take them
to meet Abasi.

"So what does your friend do out here?" Emily asked her parents as they walked out of the cool airport and into the blaze of the sun. It was so hot and bright! Emily blinked, breathing in the warm air.

"He's in charge of a project that monitors elephants," her dad told her. "I said we'd meet him at his work place."

"Cool!" said Emily.

They piled into the taxi and set off through the busy streets. Emily stared out of the window, taking it all in. There was a real mixture of people, from smartly dressed men in suits and women talking into mobile phones to scruffy teenage boys dressed in old shorts and women in traditional dress selling fruit on street corners.

At last they reached the WWF building where Abasi worked. Mr Oliver helped unload the bags and then they went inside

the cool, air-conditioned building. Emily
felt a delicious chill settle on her skin,
chasing away the heat from the sun outside.
It was quiet inside the building too, nothing
like the noisy bustling streets outside.

A Kenyan man dressed
in beige trousers and
a white shirt was
waiting for them in
the lobby. Seeing
the Olivers, he
threw his arms wide
and beamed. "Mike
and Heather, welcome!
And this must be little Emily! You have
grown so much! *Jambo!*"

Emily glanced uncertainly at her mum
and dad. What did he mean?

"It's a Swahili greeting," Mrs Oliver
explained, smiling. "Swahili is one of the
languages spoken in Kenya. It means hello.

You just say jambo back."

"*Jambo*," said Emily.

She was rewarded with another huge beam from Abasi. "It is wonderful to see you after so long. You liked the animals when you were younger, Emily."

"Well, that hasn't changed at all!" Mr Oliver said. "Emily's animal mad."

"Excellent!" Abasi nudged Emily. "Tomorrow we shall go out onto the Mara. You'll see lots of animals there. Beautiful animals – zebras, gazelle, giraffes, maybe lions . . ."

"Elephants?" said Emily hopefully.

"Elephants too. There's a herd of elephants living in the area where we'll be camping. We can try and track them. They're used to people so you should be able to get as close as you like. But for now, come with me and have something to drink."

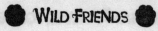

Abasi took them to a large white cafeteria in the building. Emily glanced at all the people. Some were having meetings, others chatting with friends or working on their laptops.

As they sat down with their drinks – lemonade for Emily and frothy coffee for the grown-ups – Emily felt a question burning inside her. "Abasi . . ."

He turned towards her enquiringly. "Yes, Emily?"

"You said we would see lots of elephants. Well . . ." The words rushed out of her.

"The last time I was here, when I was little, Mum and Dad said I made friends with an elephant called Kihari. Do you think we'll see her tomorrow?"

"Ah, yes . . . Kihari." Abasi's face grew troubled.

Emily felt her insides turn over. "What?"

she asked. "Has something happened to Kihari?"

"We hope not," said Abasi. "But she has disappeared. She was with her herd until a couple of weeks ago, but hasn't been seen since."

Emily's mum reached for Emily's hand. "What do you think has happened to her, Abasi?"

Abasi sighed. "We do not know. Adult elephants are rarely killed by other animals. Kihari was strong and healthy and had no obvious signs of illness, but it is unusual for an elephant to wander off from its herd for so long. Still, Kihari is an unusual elephant. She has always been on the edge of the herd, reserved and shy."

"Orphaned elephants are often outsiders

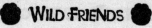

in their herds, aren't they?" Mrs Oliver said. "And Kihari was orphaned?"

"Yes, her mother was killed by poachers," Abasi said. "I hope she is alive somewhere and that poachers haven't got her too."

"Poachers?" Emily felt sick. Poachers were people who killed animals so that they could sell their fur or skin – or in the case of elephants, their ivory tusks. Ivory was worth a lot of money.

"Has there been much poaching activity recently?" Mr Oliver asked.

"There are always poachers," Abasi said with a sigh. "We try and protect the animals as best we can within the reserve, and most of the time we are successful, but people need the money and so they sometimes find a way."

Emily couldn't bear the thought of any animal being killed by poachers, let alone

the beautiful elephant she had seen in the
photograph.

Her mum squeezed her fingers. "Try
not to think about it, love. We don't know
for sure that that's what has happened to
Kihari. Hopefully she'll be safe and sound
somewhere."

Emily nodded.

"So who will we be going out on safari
with tomorrow?" Mr Oliver asked. "Or will
it be just us?"

"We'll be with Kathy, one of the vets
involved in the monitoring programme,
as well as a guide and a driver," Abasi
explained.

"Does Sami still work here?" asked Mrs
Oliver.

"No, he is now in Mozambique."

The conversation moved on as the adults
started talking about other people who
worked at WWF's Kenyan office. Emily

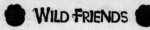
played with the straw in her lemonade.
Her thoughts were full of Kihari. She
thought of the photo of the elephant
tickling her tummy with her trunk. Why
had she disappeared?

Oh, Kihari, please be OK, Emily thought
anxiously. *Please!*

Off on Safari!

After spending the night at Abasi's flat, the Olivers got up at the crack of dawn the next day. A minibus came to collect them. It had a roof hatch that could open and a cool box with drinks in.

"This is brilliant!" said Emily, climbing up onto one of the seats and looking through the hatch. She got back down and strapped herself into her seat. There were three other people

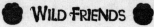

with them – the driver, who was called
Kwasi, a Masai guide from the reserve, who
was called Halisi, and Kathy, the vet.

"I've been monitoring the elephant
population in this part of the reserve for
WWF," Kathy told Emily. "We've been
trying to keep track of how many new
babies there are. It's important to know
whether the number of elephants is going
up or down so that we know how much
help and protection they need. What
animals are you most looking forward to
seeing today, Emily?"

"Definitely the elephants," Emily said.

"Another elephant fan!" said Kathy with
a smile. "I love them too. I have to say, my
job is like a dream come true."

Emily grinned. She could see why.

The jeep started and they headed off
out of Nairobi. The sky was a clear blue
with just a few wisps of white cloud. They

passed boys selling fruit and water from the
roadsides and saw people herding skinny
white cows into fields. Soon the chaos
of Nairobi turned into stretches of open
plain. As they drove, they passed through

small towns with markets and local people
watching them go by. The adults chatted.
Emily sat near Kwasi, who told her the
names of each town and pointed out things

to her – a herd of
creamy monkeys in
a thorn tree, and a
giant stork-like bird
flying through the
blue sky.

After a few hours
the road got smaller
and bumpier. Emily
had to hang on tight as they bumped and
bounced around the potholes.

Kwasi flashed a grin at her. "The jeep
has to dance on these roads but Kwasi
knows the best way. You no worry!"

Finally they reached the large security
gates that led into the reserve. "This is
one of the best-known wildlife reserves in

Kenya," Mr Oliver said to Emily. "There are a huge number of animals here and lots of people come on safari to see them. Here in the reserve the rangers can protect the animals from poachers."

"But not all the time," Emily said sadly, thinking of Kihari's mother – and maybe Kihari too.

"No," agreed Mrs Oliver. "But they do their best."

The reserve stretched out in front of them, wide grassy plains with a hazy blue sky above spotted with the occasional tree. In the distance, Emily could see some zebras grazing. She sucked in her breath. She didn't

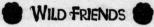

think she had seen so many at any one time. There must have been at least fifty of them!

They headed out across the grassland, the jeep bumping over the grass and sending up clouds of red dust. It was getting hotter now and Emily enjoyed the feeling of the wind in her face as they drove. As they got closer to the grazing animals she saw that as well as the stripy black and white zebras, there were slender deer-like antelope and grazing wildebeest with silvery brown coats, long faces and upturned horns. Emily didn't know where to look. There were just so many animals to see!

"Look over there," her mum said quickly.

Emily turned and saw three tall giraffes walking across the plain, their long necks bobbing as they walked. "Oh, wow!" she gasped.

"You'll get so used to seeing giraffes and zebras over the next couple of days that it'll

be just like seeing a herd of cows or a flock
of sheep back home," said her dad.

But Emily didn't think she'd ever get used
to seeing giraffes – or zebras, wildebeest and
antelope, for that matter!

"What are they?" she asked as two small
deer-like animals bounded out of the long
grass near the jeep.

"Dik dik," said Abasi.

"They're a very small kind of antelope,"

Kathy explained. "They always seem to be
in pairs, and it is said that if one of them
dies, the other won't eat or drink until it
dies too."

Emily felt a little sad at the thought as she watched the two shy creatures bound away, losing themselves in the long grass again.

They drove on until Halisi stiffened. He said something to Abasi and pointed to the west. Emily couldn't see what it was that he was looking at – it just looked like a clump of rocks and some bushes – but Abasi immediately nodded and spoke to Kwasi, who headed the jeep in that direction.

As they got closer they slowed down, and Emily saw the animals that Halisi's sharp eyes had spotted. Cheetahs! Three of them – a mother and two cubs. A little way off from the grazing animals, the mother was sitting on a rocky outcropping, her spotted body blending in with the colours around her. The two cubs were playing together. The mother cheetah looked at

the jeep, but didn't seem scared. She yawned
and looked away, as if bored.

"They see so many jeeps, most of the
animals just ignore them," Kathy said.
Kwasi stopped the jeep and Emily watched
in delight as the two cubs chased each other
around and wrestled in the grass, growling
and meowing in play. Her mum took lots of
photos.

Suddenly the mother cheetah stood up.
She stared into the distance, just like Halisi
had when he'd spotted the cheetah family.
Then Emily saw what she was looking at –
a young gazelle had wandered away from
its herd, some way off. The mother cheetah

left her cubs and started stalking towards
the baby gazelle, her head lowered, her eyes
fixed on her prey, the tip of her tail just
moving slightly.

Emily swallowed. She knew that cheetahs
needed to kill other animals in order to

survive, but she wasn't sure that she wanted
to see it. The cheetah was closing in. But
all of a sudden one of the gazelle called to
the baby. It realized how far it had come,
turned and galloped back to the safety of
its herd. The mother cheetah flicked her tail
crossly, glared after the gazelle and then
turned and loped back to her cubs.

Emily breathed a sigh of relief. The cheetah cubs ran to greet their mum and she licked them and lay down. They jumped on top of her playfully, crawling on her tummy as she rolled onto her back.

"Let's leave them to play," said Abasi with a smile, and they drove on.

Being Watched

On they went, driving past lots more
grazing animals, more cheetahs, monkeys
swinging through trees and even a
sleepy pride of lions – but to Emily's
disappointment, they didn't see any
elephants. Halisi was incredible, though. He
seemed to just *know* where animals were.
He would stiffen, say something to Kwasi
in Swahili, and off they would go across the
grassland to see something he had spotted
from far away. Abasi explained that he had
grown up on the reserve, living in one of the
Masai villages.

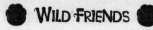

"He knows everything there is to know about animals, don't you, Halisi?"

Halisi smiled, but said nothing. He seemed to speak very little.

"It is unusual that we haven't seen elephants so far," Abasi added, frowning. "Still, we've got plenty of time this afternoon."

Finally they reached their campsite at midday. It was a small group of cream tents in the shade of some trees and near a river. Each tent had a sleeping area with mesh sides and an awning with a couple of chairs, as well as an attached toilet. In front of the tents was a table next to a ring of stones where the campfire would be made in the evening. A cook and a guard were there already. They had been getting the campsite ready for the Olivers' and Kathy's arrival.

"This campsite is used for safari holidays during the migration season," Abasi explained as they started to unload the bags. "People come and stay here to watch

the herds of animals as they all cross the
plains together in July and October to get
to new pasture. We use it when there aren't
any visitors here and we need to stay out
overnight."

Emily nodded as she took in her
surroundings. Emily and her parents were
all sleeping in one tent together. There
were three blue metal camp beds with thin
striped quilts and a rug on the floor.

"Will we be safe in a tent?" Emily asked her dad as she put her bag down beside her little bed. There was no fence or anything around the campsite. She thought of the lions they had passed. What if they decided to pay them a visit?

"We'll be fine. One of the guards will always be on watch," her dad reassured her. "We'll also light a fire which will keep the animals away. People often sleep under canvas when they're on safari. It's an incredible experience to hear the sounds of the African wildlife all around you."

Emily nodded, feeling relieved. She couldn't wait to sleep outside under the stars, but she liked to know that she was going to be safe.

Her dad grinned. "Hey, Em. How do you know when there's an elephant under your bed?"

She raised her eyebrows. Not another of

her dad's jokes. "How?"

"Your nose touches the ceiling!"

"Daaaad! That's not even funny!" Shaking her head, Emily tightened her ponytail and went outside. The sun was now beating down outside and even in the shade it was very hot. Emily saw her mum taking some pictures of a baboon in a nearby tree. He stared at her and then whisked away through the branches, showing his blue bottom.

Mrs Oliver laughed. "I don't think I'll take a photo of that."

Emily giggled and looked around. "So

what are we going to do now?"

"We'll have lunch here and rest and then go out when it gets cooler again," her mum said. "The animals all take shelter from the sun in the heat of the day. The best time to see them is in the morning and evening."

They had a delicious lunch of beef and pea stew with chapati bread, followed by big slices of fresh papaya and guava. Then they rested in their tent. Emily was keen to get out again so she was relieved when a couple of hours later they were getting back into the minibus and setting off.

"Now, we shall try and find you some elephants," Abasi said to Emily. "The herd of elephants that Kihari is usually part of often visits a watering hole near here. If we go there, we may see them."

Emily felt very excited as they headed to the watering hole. It was a large lake with thick grass around it and trees on one side. When they got there they found a herd of wildebeest and gazelle drinking there, and some funny warthogs like hairy pigs splashing around in the muddy shallows. There were also hippos bathing there – but to Emily's disappointment, there were no elephants.

Take a look at some of the pictures that inspired this story

An Indian elephant bathing.

African elephants are the largest animals to live on land.

Elephants use mud and water to cool down.

Splashing around!

An African elephant crossing the river at sunset.

Indian elephant (Elephas maximus bengalensis); Malaysia Asian elephants. Elephas maximus. In rain forest. Malay Peninsula. Malaysia. © Gerald S. Cubitt / WWF

A group of Indian elephants on the move.

Indian elephant and young Indian elephant and young (Elephas maximus) © David Lawson / WWF

An elephant cow and her calf, just like Kihari and Emily!

"Maybe they will come in a while," said Abasi.

"And in the meantime, just look at all these animals," said Mrs Oliver. They drove up as close as they could without scaring the animals away and she started to take pictures of the warthogs. The babies were particularly cute, little brown piglets who scampered around, their curly tails waggling.

Emily watched from the jeep as her mum went closer to take some more photos from different angles. Kwasi was standing at the front of the jeep, his eyes constantly scanning the surrounding grassland, watching for any signs of lions or other dangerous animals. But the watering hole stayed quiet and peaceful.

"I love the hippos," said Emily to her dad as they watched a roly-poly hippo sink down in the water until only its eyes could be seen. "I wish I could stroke one."

"There's no chance of that," her dad said. "Hippos can be really dangerous. They might look cute but they are actually quite aggressive. You wouldn't want to go into the water with one. Their teeth and jaws are incredibly strong."

As Emily continued to watch the hippos, she suddenly had the strangest feeling that

she was being watched herself. She looked
over her shoulder into the trees. Something
very large seemed to move for a moment in
the shadows. Emily peered closer. Whatever
it was, it was very big. Was it an elephant?
But now the shadows were still again. If
it was an elephant it had retreated further
into the trees.

She turned back to the watering hole,
but the feeling that she was somehow being
watched didn't leave her. Every so often
she would look back, but she never saw
anything there.

In the end they gave up on seeing
elephants and took to
driving on again.
They saw a lioness
standing on the
fallen trunk of a tree
staring hungrily at
some wildebeest, and

then a bit later, a large buffalo. It was like a very large cow with a grumpy face and huge flat horns.

"We'll see a lot of buffalo on this trip," said Abasi. "They're one of the Big Five."

"The Big Five?" questioned Emily.

"The five animals most people want to tick off on their safari list," Abasi explained. "Buffalo is the most common. Then there's rhino, leopard, elephant and lion. We shouldn't get too close to that buffalo, though. They have been known to charge vans and jeeps."

Kwasi skirted around the buffalo and they drove on.

By the time they got back to their campsite, the night was drawing in. Little kerosene lanterns had been lit and hung around the tents, casting a cheerful glow. There were still some antelope drinking at the river

near the camp. They were all hungry, so
they sat down at the table to eat a beef
stew that had been cooked slowly over the
fire, and a salad of fresh tomatoes, onions
and a green vegetable called kale. They
finished with more fresh fruit and then
sat around, chatting. At first they talked
about animals, but the conversation turned
towards people Abasi and Emily's parents

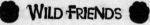

knew. Growing bored, she went over to where Halisi was keeping watch, staring out into the trees a little way off from the fire.

He smiled at her but didn't say anything, just went back to watching. Emily didn't mind the silence at all. Her head was full of images from the day and it was good just to sit peacefully, thinking of all the animals she had seen, and listening to the comforting buzz of her parents' voices behind her and the river flowing nearby. She had learned so much from this trip already.

The sky was dark now. Emily could see the Milky Way stretched across it – a banner of tiny stars that twinkled like a thick, glittering mist. Out beyond the camp she could hear the whoops and cries and hoots of different animals. As she stared out into the darkness she had the same feeling she'd had earlier – that she was being watched. She heard the crack of twigs and stiffened. Was something there?

Halisi nudged her and nodded towards the trees. "Elephant," he said softly.

"Out there?" Emily said in delight.

"Yes. Just one. It is quiet. It watches us but it will pass by."

Emily saw the shadows move. She wished she could see the elephant. Then she heard a faint noise, a gentle trumpeting. She looked at Halisi, her eyes wide.

"The elephant. I think it says *jambo*," he said with a smile.

Emily couldn't resist. She made the noise back – a soft trumpeting sound.

The sound came again – soft and gentle – and then there was the sound of branches cracking as the

elephant moved away.

Halisi watched intently for a few moments. "It has gone," he said.

Emily felt a flash of disappointment.

Halisi seemed to understand. "We see more elephants tomorrow. We get up early. They will come to drink at the river. Maybe this elephant will be there."

Later on, as Emily lay in her camp bed listening to the noises outside, she thought about the elephant in the trees. One elephant, all alone. She knew it was stupid, but part of her wanted to believe it was

Kihari, that she had come to find Emily
and show her that she was OK.

*But even if it was her, she wouldn't remember
me*, she thought to herself. *Not after all this
time.* But as she went to sleep a little bit of
her wouldn't give up hope that her friend
was nearby, safe and well.

Elephant Fun!

When Emily woke up the next day, she couldn't remember where she was. Then, as she stretched out her arms and touched the canvas of the tent, she smiled. Kenya of course!

She sat up. Her mum and dad's beds were empty. They must already be up. She heard muffled crashes and people calling out from outside. What was going on? Jumping out of bed, she went to the tent entrance. The door flaps had been pulled back. She stopped in astonishment. There were several elephants in the trees, a little way off from the campsite. They were feeding on the leaves and pulling down branches with their trunks. They looked enormous!

"Visitors!" her mum said, hurrying over. "Get dressed. We're going to go down to the river and watch them bathe!"

Emily dashed back into the tent and pulled on some shorts, a T-shirt and a hat as quickly as she could. Then she ran back outside and hurried down to the nearby river with her parents, Kwasi, Kathy and Abasi. Emily stared in delight. Three baby elephants were splashing around in the muddy water while two adults watched them. There was a loud trumpeting noise

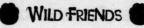

and the elephants who had been eating near the campsite appeared, their feet thumping into the ground as they walked heavily down to the water.

"Oh, wow!" breathed Emily, feeling lost for words. Ten elephants! Their great coats were covered with dry brown mud, their huge ears flapped constantly to keep away the flies and they waved their trunks. She

watched as one of the youngsters put its trunk in the river and then sprayed brown water over its back. The smallest elephant was trying to clamber out, but its feet kept slipping on the bank and it slid back into the water again and again. Eventually two of the adult elephants got into the water and pushed it out with their heads. The baby looked very funny scrambling around on the slippy mud.

Halisi caught her eye and smiled. "See," he said. "I told you, we would see elephants."

"What do you think?" Emily's dad asked her.

"They're wonderful!" Emily said happily.

Her mum had her camera out taking photos and Kathy was taking notes. Emily turned to Abasi, who was watching the elephants with a beam on his face. "Is this Kihari's herd?" she asked him.

"Yes." His face darkened. "But she is not here. She is still missing."

Emily felt a wave of sadness. What had happened to her old friend?

The older elephants started to wade into the cool water too. The river was deep and wide. The big elephants kept walking into it until they were completely under the water

with only their trunks sticking up above the surface. "Look at that!" Emily exclaimed.

"They breathe though their trunks," said her dad, putting an arm around her shoulders. "Elephants love water."

"What about the hippos?" said Emily, shading her eyes and seeing some hippos further down the river.

"Hippos and elephants generally avoid each other," her dad explained.

"Then can we go closer to the elephants?" Emily asked longingly.

"I don't think so. As lovely as elephants are, they can be dangerous," her dad said. "They can charge unexpectedly, and you certainly don't want to be on the wrong end of an elephant charge!"

Abasi overheard. "These elephants are actually very friendly. They are used to people coming here and watching them. We can certainly go closer if Emily wants to."

"Oh, yes please!" she gasped.

They walked down to the river bank while Halisi stayed back and kept a watch out for any predators approaching the river. The largest elephant made a trumpeting *haroo* noise, but it sounded friendly.

Emily copied. The elephant raised its trunk and waggled its ears and then made the sound again.

"She wants to be friends." Abasi smiled.

Emily felt the ground shake and looked around to see the smallest of the babies approaching her. It waved its little trunk at her.

"He wants to be friends too!" she said in delight.

The baby was small compared to the adult elephants, but still about as big as a small horse. He stopped in front of Emily. She put out her hand, remembering that baby elephants were called calves. The

elephant touched her fingers with his trunk
and then moved it up to her face. She stood
still while he explored her cheek and nose
and hair, huffing out as he did so.

Then he made a humming noise.
Holding her breath, she stepped closer and
stroked his leathery cheek. The elephant let
her stroke him all over, pushing his cheek
against her hand.

"It's just like seeing you with Kihari," her dad said, smiling.

Emily felt sad. If only Kihari was there with her herd, everything would be perfect.

The baby elephant put his trunk to her nose and then ambled back to the river. He looked back at her, as if expecting her to follow.

"Can I go with him?" Emily asked.

"Yes, but no going into the river," her dad said. "The current is strong and there are hippos and crocodiles upstream. You don't want to be swept away and end up with them!"

"I'll be careful," Emily promised.

She followed the baby down to the river and stood on the edge of the steep muddy bank as he slipped and slid into the water. The river was deep and came up to the baby's chin. He splashed around with his trunk, stamping his feet. Water splashed up over Emily and she gasped as the cold droplets hit her skin. The elephant looked at her and then, with a gleam in his eye, ducked his trunk into the water. Pulling it out, he shot a stream of water at Emily. It hit her in the tummy. She shrieked and staggered backwards, but as she did so, her feet slipped.

"Whoa!" she gasped as she fell over. The mud was so slippery that she started to slide down the steep bank towards the water. She tried to grab onto something, but there was

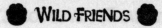

nothing there but mud. She couldn't stop
herself!

"Emily!" she heard her dad shout in
alarm as she splashed into the river.

The cool muddy water closed over her
head. It was a shock, but she didn't panic.
Kicking hard, she righted herself and
surfaced. "I'm OK!" she called, waving to
her dad.

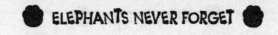
But even as she spoke, she felt the
treacherous current grab her legs like a
giant hand. It started to pull her along,
sweeping her away. She kicked and
thrashed with her arms but she was like a
twig caught in a stream. Fear rose inside her
as she tried to keep her head above water.

"Help!" she yelled as she was carried
away. "Mum! Dad! Help!"

Danger!

Emily swept past the baby elephant. She could hear her parents shouting and the elephants trumpeting. What was she going to do? She couldn't stop! What if she reached the hippos and the crocodiles?

Suddenly an adult elephant came lumbering out from the trees behind the river. It plunged down the bank into the river and stuck out its trunk. Emily banged into it but the elephant's trunk stayed firm. It was like a barrier, stopping the river from taking her. She clutched onto it. The elephant was staring at her with familiar

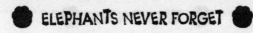

dark eyes. As their gazes met, Emily felt her
heart miss a beat.

"Kihari," she whispered. She knew
without doubt that it was her friend. She
saw the recognition in the elephant's eyes.

For a moment the world seemed to stop
– the noise, the commotion, everything
faded away. All Emily could think about
was the elephant looking at her. How?
Why? Where had she been? What was she
doing there?

Then, very gently, Kihari tugged her
towards the river bank. Emily
reached the bank, her
hands sinking into
the gooey mud.

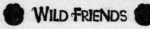
Kihari lowered her head into the water and nudged Emily gently, helping her up just as the adult elephants had done with the calf before. Emily scrambled up the slope. Her mum and dad kneeled down and helped to pull her to safety.

"Oh, Emily!" her mum gasped, hugging her close. "I'm so glad you're OK!"

Emily felt her dad's arms fold around her too. Relief rushed through her. She was safe. She suddenly realized how scared she'd been. But she had been rescued.

"Kihari!" she breathed. "She saved me."

She swung around and saw the elephant watching her.

"Kihari?" Mrs Oliver said in surprise.

Abasi and Kathy had joined them. "Emily is right. That elephant is Kihari," Kathy said, checking her notes. "She's got a slight chip in one tusk and a dark mark on her right ear."

"But you thought she was missing," said Mrs Oliver.

"She was," Kathy explained. "But it seems she has come back."

The elephant was still staring at Emily. She made a low trumpeting sound: *haroo*. Emily recognized it from the night before in the dark. She pulled free from her mum and

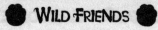

dad and made the noise back. The elephant lifted her trunk in reply.

"It was you," Emily realized. "Last night. You were watching me in the trees by the camp." She remembered the feeling she'd had of being watched that morning, and the day before. Kihari must have been in the trees. "You've been watching me since we got here."

Emily felt her stomach tighten. She knew it sounded silly, but might Kihari have remembered her?

The elephant waded out of the water, brown mud coating her grey wrinkled body. She flapped her ears. Emily went up to her and Kihari lowered her head. Emily stroked her. "Thank you."

Kihari lifted her trunk to Emily's face and blew out gently, then she prodded Emily's tummy, as she had in the photo. Emily giggled.

"What's this about her watching you?"
said Mrs Oliver.

Emily explained. Halisi, who was
listening, nodded. "Elephant was there," he
said.

"But why has she been in the trees?"
said Mr Oliver, mystified. "Why's she been
hiding?"

They all looked at each other in
confusion.

Giving Emily one last nuzzle, Kihari lumbered off towards the trees. She trumpeted loudly. Seconds later there was a high pitched noise that sounded like someone blowing badly down a tuba, and then a very young baby elephant appeared between the tree trunks.

"She's had a calf!" exclaimed Kathy.

Abasi beamed. "So she hasn't been missing from her herd at all! She must have just wanted some peace and quiet to have her baby!"

Kihari's calf was the cutest thing Emily thought she had ever seen. She was like a perfect miniature version of Kihari, right down to the dark spot on her ear. She stepped out shyly into the sunlight, looking around with curious dark eyes. Kihari touched her with her trunk, then looked at Emily, as if to say, 'Come and say hello!'

Emily went forward slowly, not wanting to alarm the baby, but she didn't seem worried at all. As Emily stopped in front of her she reached out with her trunk. Emily could hardly believe it as she petted her. Kihari and a brand new baby elephant – she felt like all her dreams had come true!

She was aware of her mum taking loads

of pictures. Abasi, Kathy and her dad stood together, smiling at her, while Halisi and Kwasi watched from the jeep. But all she could really think about were the two elephants in front of her. Her very first wild friend, and now a brand new little wild friend too.

"Emily! Turn this way!" her mum called. Emily turned for the camera and smiled, her arm over the calf's back. Her mum snapped a photo.

The other elephants had noticed the baby and started to come over. Emily decided to leave them to get acquainted with the baby under Kihari's watchful eye.

She ran over to join her parents and they watched as the other elephants all greeted the baby by touching her with their trunks.

"Adult female elephants in a herd often take it in turns to look after each others' babies," her dad explained. "They cherish any new arrival."

Emily smiled. It was almost like watching a group of human aunts crowding around a human baby.

The calf waved her little trunk cheekily at her new relatives.

"We'll have to think of a name for her," said Abasi.

Kathy smiled. "I think she should be called Emily."

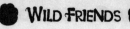

Mr Oliver chuckled. "Hmm. Emily the elephant. It certainly has a ring to it. What do you think, Em?"

"I love it!" Emily grinned. It felt like a weight had dropped off her shoulders now that she knew Kihari was safe – and she still had two days of safari left. What could be better than that?

"I've got some great photos of you and little Emily and Kihari," said her mum. "You'll be able to show everyone at school."

"And you'll be able to tell them how you got rescued by an elephant. Not many people can say that," her dad added.

"I still can't believe Kihari jumped in and helped me," said Emily, awed at how amazing the elephant had been.

Her mum put her arm around her shoulders. "I guess it's true what they say, love – elephants never forget."

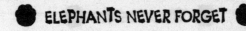

"Do you think?" Emily looked at Kihari, reunited with the herd as they fussed over her baby. "Thank you, Kihari," she said softly. She knew no matter how many more animals she saw, she would also never forget her.

The elephant's eyes met hers across the grass – dark, twinkling and wise – and Emily smiled.

Over the next couple of days Emily saw more animals than she could even have dreamed of. They visited a Masai village and even managed to track and see a leopard, the most rarely spotted of the Big Five animals. They went out one night for a night-time safari and saw the cutest little

bush babies with enormous dark eyes. Every
morning they got up at dawn and went to
check on Kihari's herd down by the river.
Emily's mum took lots and lots of photos,
but Emily's favourite photo by far was the
one of her with Kihari and little Emily.

"Will you print it out for me when we
get back home so I can put it up in my
room?" she asked her mum when they were
finally sitting on the aeroplane waiting to
take off and fly back to England.

"Of course I will," her mum said.

"I love Kenya," Emily said, looking out

of the window. "I really want to come back here and see Kihari and the other elephants one day."

"Hopefully you will," her mum replied.

"Hey, Em." Her dad nudged her. "We're in a plane – what do you call an elephant that flies?"

"What?" asked Emily.

"A jumbo jet!" Her dad chuckled.

Emily and her mum exchanged looks and shook their heads. "The elephant jokes are one thing I won't miss about Kenya!" Emily's mum said.

The plane had started to move along the runway. Emily looked out of the window as they got faster and faster. *One day I will come back and see Kihari and Emily again*, she promised herself.

As the plane took off into the blue sky, Emily wondered what adventures she would have had by the time she came back, and

what other animals she would have met.
She hugged her arms around herself. She
couldn't wait to find out!

Read on for lots of amazing
elephant facts, fun puzzles
and more about WWF

WWF

Elephant Fact File

Best feature: Their long trunks are an extension of their upper lip and nose.
They have two finger-like points at the end of their trunks that they use for grabbing things.

Size: They are 3m tall and weigh up to 6 tonnes – making them the largest land mammal on Earth.

Favourite food: They are herbivores, and eat roots, grasses and bark. They need to eat a couple of hundred kilogrammes of plant matter a day!

Home: They are savannah elephants and live in grassy plains and woodlands.

Current population: Around 600,000 African elephants and only 41–52,000 Asian elephants live in the wild.

Breeding and family: Elephants are social animals with strong family ties. Cows (females) and their calves, live in family units under the leadership of a mature female. Young bulls (males) are driven from the family when they reach puberty to live in separate bachelor herds. Adult bulls live alone and join a family unit only briefly when a female is ready to mate. Elephants mate when they are 12 to 15 years old. Courtship involves a display of affection between the cow and bull in which they caress each other with their trunks. A single calf, standing about 33 inches high and weighing approximately 250 pounds is born 22 months later.

Life span: An African elephant's average life span is about 60-65 years.

Biggest threat: Poachers who hunt them for their ivory tusks.

Bonus fact: Their trunks have around 150,000 muscles!

Quiz time!

1. How do you say hello in Swahili?

2. What is the name of the nature reserve that the Olivers' visit in Kenya?

3. What colour is the baboon's bottom that Mrs Oliver takes a picture of?

4. What is a baby elephant called?

5. What is the name of the driver who takes the Olivers' on safari?

6. How long was Emily's flight to Nairobi?

Jambo, Masai Mara, blue, calf, Kwasi, 8 hours

Word Search

Reading across, up, down and diagonally,
see if you can find all the listed words
in the grid below . . .

B	A	D	E	C	H	E	E	T	A	H	U	P
I	W	Q	A	D	D	R	I	X	Z	V	K	Y
O	H	R	S	J	X	G	F	Q	O	W	E	O
R	I	V	W	A	Q	Z	I	J	G	L	N	X
S	P	X	J	M	S	H	L	R	J	Q	Y	J
D	P	E	Q	X	B	X	W	U	A	X	A	Q
V	O	Z	M	Q	I	J	Q	H	M	F	L	P
I	Q	X	I	Z	R	F	G	H	B	I	A	O
T	W	E	U	Q	U	I	Y	R	O	T	I	S
Y	Q	W	R	H	F	D	V	P	H	L	O	U
P	S	Z	T	N	A	H	P	E	L	E	G	F
O	N	B	E	E	X	W	T	Y	R	L	O	U
Y	K	N	U	R	T	D	F	L	Q	Z	E	E

ELEPHANT   **KENYA**   **CHEETAH**   **TRUNK**

JAMBO   **HIPPO**   **RIVER**   **SAFARI**

Spot the Difference

Can you spot the five differences
between these two elephant pictures?

Answers: 1. Monkey on the tree stump 2. Missing tree branch on left-hand tree 3. Calf's tail missing 4. Tusk chipped 5. Extra leaves on cut-off tree trunk in foreground

Word Scramble

The names of these characters from
the book are all jumbled up.
Can you unscramble them?

IAHKIR

⬜⬜⬜⬜⬜⬜

BIAAS

⬜⬜⬜⬜⬜

LHASII

⬜⬜⬜⬜⬜⬜

YIMEL

⬜⬜⬜⬜⬜⬜

WIKSA

⬜⬜ ⬜⬜⬜⬜⬜⬜

More about WWF

You're probably familiar with WWF's panda logo,
but did you know that WWF . . .

- Is the world's leading conservation organization.

- Was set up in 1961 (when TV was still black and white!).

- Works with lots of different people around the world, including governments, businesses and individuals, to make a difference to the world we live in.

- Is a charity and most of their money comes from members and supporters.

WWF's aim

The planet is our most precious resource and we need to take care of it! WWF want to build a future where people live in harmony with nature.

WWF are working towards this by:

 Protecting the natural world.

 Helping to limit climate change and find ways to help people deal with the impacts of it.

 Helping to change the way we live, so that the world's natural resources (like water and trees) are used more carefully, so they last for future generations.

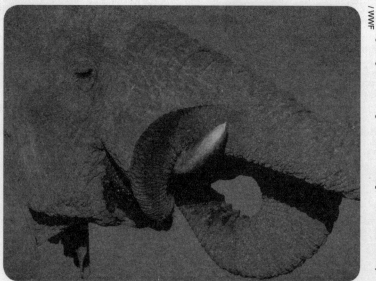

African elephants (Loxodonta africana sp.) African elephant, Loxodonta africana, greeting and interacting with trunks touching. Africa © Martin Harvey / WWF

What do WWF do?

Conservation – Protect rare species of wild animals and plants as well as important ecosystems found in forests, rivers and seas.

Climate change – They don't just tackle the causes of global warming, but also the impacts of climate change on communities and environments.

Sustainability – Help to change the way we all live, particularly in richer developed countries like the UK, including decisions about what we eat, buy and use for fuel.

How can I help WWF?

There are lots of ways you can take action in your own home to help protect our beautiful planet and the people and animals that live on it. Here are a few ideas to get you started . . .

Buy sustainable

One of the biggest threats to a lot of wildlife, including the giant panda, is loss of habitat. This is often from people cutting down trees to use in paper or wood products, or to make way for roads, and clearing areas to use for farming.

You can help stop this by only buying products that are sustainably farmed, or wood and paper products from sustainable forests.

So when you're out shopping with your mum or dad, look for:

 Certified paper and wood products (look for the FSC logo to tell if something is certified or not)

 Products made from certified sustainable palm oil (look for the RSPO logo to be sure that they are certified)

If your local shops don't stock these products – ask them why!

Reduce, reuse, recycle!

Households in the UK send 18 million tonnes of rubbish to landfill yearly. That's more than any other country in Europe!

Top five tips to reduce waste

Why don't you do some of these over a week and see how much less rubbish you throw away than normal?

Take a reuseable bag when you go to the shops, instead of picking up a new one.

Take any clothes, shoes, books or toys you don't want any more to a charity shop.

Clean out old food jars and pots to use for storage.

Get creative with your rubbish and make a kitchen-roll penguin.

Make postcards by cutting old birthday and Christmas cards in half, and give them to your friends.

"Go Wild!"

The way we live can affect people, wildlife and habitats all around the world. Making small but important changes to the way we act really can help to save polar bears in the Arctic or orang-utans in Borneo and Sumatra.

And this is what the Go Wild club is all about. It's your chance to learn more about some of the animals and habitats that we're working to protect. It's also about discovering what you can do in your own home to help look after the natural world.

By joining WWF's Go Wild club at *wwf.org.uk/gowildjoin*, you will recieve a member's pack and magazines that will take you on an incredible journey around the world, meeting some amazing animals and individuals. You'll find out what life's like for them and the threats they face to their environments.

As well as getting lots of Go Wild goodies, being a member means that you help WWF to continue their work. Join today and explore your wild side!

Don't miss Emily's adventure with lovable baby orang-utan Koyah, in the next Wild Friends story, ORANG-UTAN ADVENTURE

Read on for a sneak peek!

Caught on Camera!

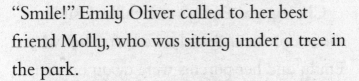

"Smile!" Emily Oliver called to her best friend Molly, who was sitting under a tree in the park.

Molly rolled her eyes. "Stop taking photos of me! You've got loads already."

"So?" said Emily, clicking the button on her new camera anyway. "I've got to practise taking photos before I go away next week."

The following week Emily and her parents were going to Borneo to see orang-utans in the wild. Emily's mum and dad both worked for WWF, an organization that

tried to protect endangered animals and
their habitats around the world. Emily's
mum had given her a camera of her own so
she could take photos while they were there.

"I wish you could come with me," Emily
sighed.

"Me too," Molly said. "But at least I get
to look after Cherry while you're away!"

Cherry was Emily's chinchilla. Usually
the people next door looked after her when
Emily and her parents were away on their
travels, but this time Molly's parents had
said she could look after the chinchilla.

"You do know all the things she likes,
don't you?" said Emily anxiously. She hated
leaving her pet. "Carrots and dried apple
chunks for treats."

"I know," said Molly. "And she loves
raisins but can't have too many of them.
She can have as many cuddles as she
wants, though. She'll be fine with me, Em. I

promise I'll look after her really well."

"Thanks," Emily said, smiling. "I know she'll love being with you."

"So why are your parents going to Borneo?" Molly asked.

"Well, Mum's going to take photos," said Emily. Her mum was a wildlife photographer. "And Dad is checking up on a project there that he's been looking after. It monitors the number of orang-utans in the forest where we're going." She remembered some of the things she had been reading about orang-utans in the last few days. "Did you know that orang-utans are one of the most intelligent animals in the world? They use tools and build nests for themselves."

"Nests?" said Molly in surprise. "They're not birds!"

"No, but they do sleep in trees, just like birds do," said Emily. "They can build a new nest in just five minutes and they have really long arms, up to two metres."

"Wow!" said Molly, looking at her own arms. "That's mega-long!"

Emily grinned. "The adult males are eight times as strong as humans, too. Just imagine that! The babies are really cute though." She pictured some of the orang-utans she had seen on the Internet. The adults were covered with long, shaggy red-brown hair, the colour of a conker fresh out of its shell. They had dark grey faces, big brown eyes and mouths that could smile or look sad. The babies were like the adults but their fur was less thick and their eyes looked massive in their little faces. "They make an OO-OO-OO noise."

Molly copied her.

"That's right," said Emily. "It's quiet when they're scared and loud when they're excited."

"So what do orang-utans do all day?" asked Molly curiously.

"Eat, mainly!" said Emily. "They love fruit and eat lots of it. But they also eat bark and seeds and insects. When they're not eating they swing through the trees from their arms."

"I can do that!" Molly grinned and jumped up. The oak tree had a sturdy branch just above her head. She jumped up and caught hold of it and then swung herself back and forward. "I'm an orang-utan!" she shouted as she hung from one arm.

Emily grinned and snapped a quick photo. "I'll show the orang-utans this and tell them I've found them a long lost cousin of theirs!"

Molly giggled and switched to the other arm. "OO-OO-OO!"

Shoving her camera in the pocket of her

jeans, Emily jumped up and grabbed the branch too. "Come on, let's play at being orang-utans!"

She swung after her friend, happiness bubbling through her. Playing with Molly was great fun but soon she would be seeing orang-utans for real!

For more fun, games and wild stories, visit wwf.org.uk/gowild

WWF